Monkey Trouble
and other grandfather stories

Ruskin Bond has been writing for over sixty years, and has now over 120 titles in print—novels, collections of stories, poetry, essays, anthologies and books for children. His first novel, *The Room on the Roof*, received the prestigious John Llewellyn Rhys Award in 1957. He has also received the Padma Shri (1999), the Padma Bhushan (2014) and two awards from the Sahitya Akademi—one for his short stories and another for his writings for children. In 2012, the Delhi government gave him its Lifetime Achievement Award.

Born in 1934, Ruskin Bond grew up in Jamnagar, Shimla, New Delhi and Dehradun. Apart from three years in the UK, he has spent all his life in India, and now lives in Mussoorie with his adopted family.

Priya Kuriyan is a children's book illustrator, comic book artist and an animator. A graduate of the National Institute of Design (Ahmedabad), she has directed educational films for *Sesame Street* (India) and the Children's Film Society of India (CFSI), and illustrated numerous children's books for various Indian publishers. She currently lives in New Delhi, filling her sketchbooks with funny caricatures of its residents. You can see her work at priyakuriyan.blogspot.com, pkuriyan.blogspot.com.

Ruskin Bond
Illustrations Priya Kuriyan

Monkey Trouble
and other grandfather stories

RED TURTLE
RUPA

Published in Red Turtle by
Rupa Publications India Pvt. Ltd 2016
7/16, Ansari Road, Daryaganj
New Delhi 110002

Sales centres:
Prayagraj Bengaluru Chennai
Hyderabad Jaipur Kathmandu
Kolkata Mumbai

Story copyright © Ruskin Bond 2016
Illustration copyright © Rupa Publications India Pvt. Ltd. 2016

This is a work of fiction. Names, characters, places and incidents are either the product of the author's imagination or are used fictitiously and any resemblance to any actual person, living or dead, events or locales is entirely coincidental.

All rights reserved.
No part of this publication may be reproduced, transmitted, or stored in a retrieval system, in any form or by any means, electronic, mechanical, photocopying, recording or otherwise, without the prior permission of the publisher.

P-ISBN: 978-81-291-3737-1
E-ISBN: 978-81-291-4358-7

Eighth impression 2023

10 9 8

The moral right of the author has been asserted.

Printed in India

This book is sold subject to the condition that it shall not, by way of trade or otherwise, be lent, resold, hired out, or otherwise circulated, without the publisher's prior consent, in any form of binding or cover other than that in which it is published.

Monkey Trouble

When Grandfather had to visit Meerut to collect his railway pension, he decided to take Tutu and me along to keep us both out of mischief.

Tutu was put in a bag to keep her from wandering about on the train and causing inconvenience to the passengers.

There was enough space for Tutu to look out of the bag occasionally and to be fed with bananas and biscuits.

Tutu's efforts to get out only had the effect of making the bag roll about on the floor or occasionally jump into the air—an exhibition that attracted a curious crowd of onlookers at the Dehradun and Meerut stations.

Eye of the Eagle

A special tree

That year the monsoon rains came early.

The tree grew quickly that season.

And looked delectable enough to be devoured by a wandering goat.